Do you have a favourite story about a truly wicked villain? Don't you love to hate those mean, bullying types? And what about when they get what's coming to them – aah! It's fun to read about a really awful person, particularly when they don't have any idea of just how awful they are!

That's why we enjoyed writing about Tashi's Uncle Tiki Pu so much, and why we missed him when we finished Tashi and the Genie.

So here he is again, back to his old tricks of looking out for himself, and causing Tashi even more trouble...

ANNA AND BARBARA FIENBERG

Anna and Barbara Fienberg write the Tashi stories together, making up all kinds of daredevil adventures and tricky characters for him to face. Lucky he's such a clever Tashi.

Kim Gamble is one of Australia's favourite illustrators for children. Together Kim and Anna have made such wonderful books as *The Magnificent Nose and Other Marvels*, *The Hottest Boy Who Ever Lived*, the *Tashi* series, the *Minton* picture books, *Joseph,* and a full colour picture book about their favourite adventurer, *There once was a boy called Tashi*.

First published in 2001
This edition first published in 2006

Allen & Unwin
83 Alexander St
Crows Nest NSW 2065
Australia
Phone: (61 2) 8425 0100
Fax: (61 2) 9906 2218
Email: info@allenandunwin.com
Web: www.allenandunwin.com

National Library of Australia
Cataloguing-in-Publication entry:

Fienberg, Anna.
    Tashi and the dancing shoes.

    New cover ed.
    For primary school children.
    ISBN 978 1 74114 972 2.

    ISBN 1 74114 972 X.

    1. Children's stories, Australian. 2. Tashi (Fictitious character) – Juvenile
    fiction. I. Fienberg, Barbara. II. Gamble, Kim. III. Title. (Series: Tashi; 8).

A823.3

Cover and series design by Sandra Nobes
Typeset in Sabon by Tou-Can Design
Printed in Australia by McPhersons Printing Group

10 9 8 7 6 5 4 3 2 1

and the
DANCING
SHOES

written by
Anna Fienberg
and
Barbara Fienberg
•

illustrated by
Kim Gamble

ALLEN&UNWIN

One Saturday, Jack invited Tashi for lunch to meet his Uncle Joe.

'He's my father's brother,' Jack told him proudly. 'He's been travelling all over the world.'

'That's interesting,' said Tashi. 'I wonder if he's ever been to *my* village.'

'We'll ask him,' Jack said excitedly. 'You can swap stories about snake-infested forests and wild escapes from war lords. It'll be great!'

Tashi and Joe did have a lot to talk about. They talked all through the soup, well into the beef with noodles, pausing only when the apple cake was served.

'It's very good to meet an uncle of yours, Jack,' said Tashi, taking a bite of his cake. 'Have you got any more?'

'There's some in the kitchen,' said Mum, hopping up.

'He meant *uncles*, Mum,' laughed Jack. 'You know, if we asked all *yours* to lunch, Tashi, we'd have to hire the town hall!'

Tashi nodded. 'It's true. But I'll tell you something. No matter if you have forty uncles and fifty-six aunts and nine hundred and two cousins, all of them are precious.' He sighed. 'Take Lotus Blossom, for example.'

'Who's that?' asked Dad, scratching his head. 'An uncle?'

Tashi scooped up the last of his cake. 'No, Lotus Blossom is my cousin. We used to play chasings near the river in summer. *Wah*, was she a fast runner! Nearly quicker than *me!* She'd go streaking off on her own then hide in the tiniest, most impossible places. I'd take ages to find her.'

Tashi finished up his cake and pushed back his chair. 'So when they told me Lotus Blossom had disappeared, I wasn't too worried. At first, that is.'

Uncle Joe leaned forward. 'Disappeared, eh?' He nodded knowingly. 'What was it? Bandits, war lords, *kid*nappers?'

Dad winked at Jack. 'Here we go!' he whispered, bouncing on his chair.

'Well, it was like this,' began Tashi.
'One afternoon, my mother and I had just
come back from a visit to Wise-as-an-Owl,
when there was a furious knocking at the
door and Lotus Blossom's grandmother,
Wang Mah, stumbled in. Her face was wet
with tears and strands of hair from her bun
were plastered across her cheeks.

'"I've lost her!" Wang Mah burst out.
"One minute my dear little Lotus Blossom
was playing in the courtyard right next to
me – the *next*, she was gone!" She wrung
her hands. "Oh, what will happen when
night falls?"

'My mother sat her down on a chair.

'"I was just painting my screen," Wang Mah went on. "You know, the one with the Red Whiskered Dragon? Well, I couldn't get the green right on the scales – "

'"Where did you look for her?" I interrupted.

'Wang Mah threw up her hands. "Oh, everywhere! The fields, the cemetery – I've told the whole village, practically. Everyone's out looking, but no one can find her. Oh, my little one, where could she be?"

'Well, I knew we wouldn't find her sitting there in the house worrying, so I told my mother that I was going to join the search party and that I would be back later.

'"Oh, thank you, Tashi," cried Wang Mah. "If anyone can find her, you will, I know."

'I wasn't so sure, but I crossed my fingers and gave her the sign of the dragon for luck. But as I walked towards the village square, a cold fear was settling in my stomach. Whenever Grandmother was painting one of her screens, she didn't hear or see anything else for hours. Lotus Blossom might have been missing since dawn. So I decided to go at once to the village fortune teller.'

Uncle Joe nodded wisely. 'I went to one last year, when I was back in the tropics. Did I ever tell you about the time – '

'Yes,' said Dad quickly.

'So, Tashi,' said Mum, 'did the fortune teller have any news?'

'Well, it was like this. Luk Ahed had done horoscope charts for everyone in our village, so I thought he might give us a clue about Lotus Blossom. Luk Ahed is very good at telling the future, but not so brilliant at keeping things tidy. He rummaged through great piles of sacred books and maps of the stars and bamboo sticks. But he couldn't find her horoscope anywhere.

'"I'll start on a new one right away,"
he promised. Then he grunted with
surprise. He had *my* chart in his hand.

'"Just look at this," he marvelled. "I see
a great adventure awaiting you, Tashi, just
as soon as you find a very special pair of
red shoes with green glass peacocks
embroidered on them."

'I walked out of there very thoughtfully, I can tell you. I could almost remember seeing such a pair of shoes, but where? As I turned the corner into the village I heard the familiar rat-a-tat-tat coming from the shoemaker's shop.

'"Hello, Tashi," Not Yet called from his open door. Our cobbler was called Not Yet because no matter how long people left their shoes with him, when they returned to see if they were ready, he always said, "Not yet. Come back later."

'Well, I stopped right there on the doorstep. Of course, *that's* where I'd seen those strange shoes. I ran into the shop and asked Not Yet if he still had them.

'"I think so," said Not Yet. "I know the ones you mean. They were here when I took over this shop from my father years ago." He poked around at the back of the shelves and finally fished out a dusty pair of shoes. He wiped them clean with his sleeve.

'The shoes were just as I remembered. They were red satin and glowed in the dingy room. I took some coins from my pocket and asked, "Could I take them now?"

'Not Yet look at the worn soles and heels and clicked his tongue. "Not yet," he said. "Come back later."

'So I went down to the river for a while and looked along the banks and in our usual hiding places for any sign of Lotus Blossom. After an hour, without a speck of dragon luck, I returned to the shop.

'"Be careful with them, Tashi," Not Yet said as he handed the shoes to me. "Be *very* careful." And he looked at me in a worried way.

'Clutching them tightly to my chest,
I ran as fast as I could to the edge of the
village. The shoes glowed like small twin
sunsets in my hand. When I stopped and
put them on, my feet began to grow hot
and tingle. I gave a little hop. At least
I meant to give a little hop, but instead
it was a great whopping *leap*, followed by
another and another, even higher. I couldn't
help laughing, it felt so strange. I ran a few
steps, but each step was a huge bound. In
a few seconds I had crossed the fields and
was down by the river again.

'Well, even though I was so worried about Lotus Blossom, I have to tell you I couldn't help being excited about the shoes.'

'Who could?' cried Dad. 'No one would blame you for that!'

'So I decided to run home – just for a minute, you know – and show my family. But those shoes had other ideas! They went on running in quite the opposite direction: over the bridge and into the forest. I tried to stop, but the shoes wouldn't let me. I tried to kick them off, but they were stuck fast to my feet. I was getting very tired, and a little bit scared.'

'Who wouldn't be?' said Dad.

'Even I, with my vast experience, would be alarmed by the situation,' put in Uncle Joe.

'Yes, and then I saw the long shadows of the trees and the deepening dusk. Soon it would be dark, and I didn't know where on earth the shoes were taking me.

'Just then I heard a shout. The shoes bounded on and stopped suddenly near the edge of a deep pit. A tiger pit! I shivered deep inside. I'd had quite enough of tigers, remember, when I was trapped with one in that wicked Baron's storeroom.'

'Old Baron *bogey*,' muttered Dad.

'A voice yelped again, "Is anyone there?" And do you know, it was Lotus Blossom!

'"Yes, it's me, Tashi!" I called, and the shoes moved forward. I leaned over the side of the pit. "Hello, Lotus Blossom. How did you come to fall down there? You weren't *hid*ing, were you?"   g,

'"No!" yelled Lotus Blossom, stamping her foot. "It's no joke being down here. I got lost, and I was running, and there were branches over the pit so you couldn't see it. Oh, Tashi, I've been here all day, so frightened that a tiger might come and fall in on top of me."

'I jerked back and shot a look over my shoulder. But what could I do? I had no rope or any means of getting her up. Then my toes tingled inside the shoes, reminding me. Yes! My splendid magic shoes could take me home in no time and I would be back with a good long rope as quick as two winks of an eye.

'But at that moment Lotus Blossom began to scream. My heart thumped as I saw a large black snake slithering down into the hole, gliding towards her.

'I didn't have time to think. The shoes picked me up and jumped me down into the pit. *Wah!*

'Maybe I'll land on the snake and squash him, I thought. But no, the snake heard me coming and slid to one side. I landed with a crash.

'"Hide behind me, Lotus Blossom," I said, facing the serpent. Lotus Blossom did as I told her, but doesn't she always have to have the last word? She picked up rocks and threw them at the snake, shouting "*WAH! PCHAAA!*"

'"Leave him, Lotus Blossom!" I whispered, but it was too late. The snake was enraged. It drove us back into the corner, lunging fiercely.

'"Put your arms around my waist and hold on," I told Lotus Blossom.

'No sooner had she done so than my feet began to tingle. The magic shoes jumped me straight up the steep side of the pit and out into the clean, fresh air.

'I hoisted Lotus Blossom onto my shoulders and with a few exciting bounds we were back in the village square. The bell was rung to call back the searchers, and you should have seen them racing joyfully towards us! They swept Lotus Blossom up into their arms, clapping and cheering like thunder. Wang Mah grabbed her, and scolded and wept, her long white hair tangling them both together. But when the crowd saw me doing one of my playful little leaps – well, *flying* right over their heads! – they gasped in amazement.

'"Look at those shoes! Where did he get them? Look at him fly!" they cried.

'I was just taking my bow when I spied a face in the crowd that I had hoped never to see again: my greedy Uncle Tiki Pu.'

'Oh, *him!*' Jack turned to Uncle Joe. 'He's the worst uncle ever. When he came to stay with Tashi, he threw all the toys out the window to make way for his things!'

'I just brought my pyjamas and a change of underpants for the weekend,' said Uncle Joe quickly. 'Is that all right?'

'When the crowd drifted away,' Tashi went on, 'I walked home. I was feeling very gloomy, muttering to myself, when suddenly Tiki Pu's shadow loomed over me. He was rubbing his hands together with glee, and my heart sank. But I needn't have worried about him coming to *stay* – that was going to be the least of my problems.

'"You must come to the city with me, Tashi," he said, gripping my shoulder hard. "I know the Emperor well. Er, not the Emperor himself, perhaps, but certainly his Master of Revels. He could arrange for you to dance at the Palace. We will make our fortunes!"

'*We* will! *Our* fortunes? I thought.

'Tiki Pu was very insistent, never letting me have any peace with all his jawing on – "imagine, the *Emperor*, the *Emperor*!" – so in the end I agreed to go.

'The next morning, Tiki Pu stood on my toes (yes, it hurt, but at least it was quick) and off we bounded. It was amazing – a journey that took days of normal walking was over in half an hour. Suddenly, there we were at the front door of the Emperor's Master of Revels.

'The Master didn't look too pleased to
see Uncle Tiki Pu. But after he had watched
me do six somersaults from one leap, and
dance up one wall, across the ceiling and
down the other side, he clapped Tiki Pu on
the shoulder.

'"The Emperor is giving a grand dinner
tonight," he said. "The boy will dance for
him at the Palace."

'"Will the Princess Sarashina be there?"
I asked.

'"No, she is away visiting her aunt," the Master of Revels called over his shoulder as he hurried away to make the arrangements. Then he stopped. I saw him look back at me, and a sly expression came over his face. His eyes narrowed into a mean smile.

'We had only gone a little way when the Master came after us. He had two huge evil-looking guards with him.

'"Take those shoes from the boy," the Master ordered. "They should fit my son perfectly. He will be much more graceful. Why should *this* clumsy oaf have the honour of dancing before the Emperor!"

'"The Master's honourable son will bring him glory and gold!" said the first guard.

'"Praise and presents!" said the second guard.

'"The shoes won't come off," I said loudly. "I've *tried*."

'The guards rushed at me and pushed and pulled, but they couldn't remove the shoes.

'"Oh, well – chop off his feet!" ordered the Master. "We can dig his toes out of the shoes later."

'I looked desperately at my uncle. Tiki Pu took a very small step forward. "Ah," he stammered. "You shouldn't really, I mean to say, that's not very – "

'"Be quiet," snapped the Master, "or we will chop off his head, and yours as well."

'Tiki Pu stepped back quickly. "Oh, in that case . . . "

'Some uncle, I thought bitterly.

'The guard drew out his mighty sword and swung it up above his head . . . But before he could bring it down, the door flew open and Princess Sarashina burst into the room.

'"What are you doing?" she cried. "Put that sword down at once. This is Tashi, the boy who rescued me from the demons and saved my life! Just as well I came back early, Tashi. What a way to repay your kindness." She scolded the Master of Revels and his guards out of the room.

'Well, I was never so glad to see anyone in my whole life. So when the Princess invited me to take tea with her, I followed her into a beautiful room all hung about with silks and tapestries, and we talked and laughed until nightfall.

'That evening I danced for the Emperor and the Court. I twirled high over people's heads and swooped and ducked and glided like a bird.

'"Miraculous!" they cried, throwing coins at me, which Uncle Tiki Pu hastily gathered up. The Emperor gave me a nice little bag of gold for my trouble, but Tiki Pu was at my side at once. He whisked the bag from my hand.

'"I'll keep this safe for you, Tashi my boy," he beamed, as he slipped it into his pocket.

'"Is there anything else I can do for you, Tashi?" the Emperor asked.

'"Not for me, your Highness, but there is something my uncle would dearly like."

'Tiki Pu pricked up his ears and gave me a toothy grin.

'"And what is that, my boy?" the Emperor smiled.

'"My uncle has always had a great desire to travel." Out of the corner of my eye I saw that Tiki Pu looked very surprised. I whispered something in the Emperor's ear.'

'What? What?' cried Dad.

'I know, I know!' cried Uncle Joe.

'Well, the next day I returned home alone and went straight at once to see Luk Ahed, the fortune teller. "You were right about the shoes," I said, "but I've had enough adventures for the time being, and I'm so tired. Can you tell me how to take them off?"

'"Nothing could be easier," said Luk Ahed. "All you have to do is twirl around three times, clap your hands and say, Off shoes!"

'I followed his instruction and oh, the relief to wiggle my toes in the cool dust. I carried the shoes home and carefully put them in the bottom of my playbox.

'"And Tiki Pu hasn't come back with you?" my mother asked when I told her about the grand dinner and the Emperor and Princess Sarashina.

'"No, he couldn't. A ship was leaving the next morning for Africa and the Emperor thought that it was too good an opportunity for Tiki Pu to miss, seeing he likes travel so much."

'My mother gave me one of her searching looks. "What a clever Tashi," she said at last, and smiled.'

There was a little silence at the table. Then Dad snorted loudly. 'Some uncle, all right, that Tiki Pu. Of all the lily-livered, cowardly . . . You wouldn't say *he* was a precious relative, would you, Tashi?'

'About as precious as a crocodile hanging off your leg!' put in Uncle Joe.

'He may have met a few by now,' grinned Tashi. 'Crocodiles are quite common in Africa, aren't they?'

'So I believe,' said Joe. 'In fact once, when I was in a typical African forest,

I saw a crocodile grab the muzzle of a zebra. Pulled him into the river, easy as blinking. Dreadful sight. A Nile crocodile, it was. Notorious man-killers. Did I tell you about the time . . . ?'

And so Tashi stayed till dusk crept in all over the table and Dad had to put the lights on and Tashi's mother called him home for dinner.

'Come back tomorrow, young fellow!' urged Uncle Joe. 'I'm cooking *crocodile!*'

THE FORTUNE TELLER

'Funny how crocodile tastes almost exactly like chicken,' remarked Dad.

'Yes, same chewy white meat,' said Mum.

Uncle Joe stared very hard at his plate. 'Actually,' he said, after a long pause, 'they were out of crocodile at the supermarket. Fancy! In Tiabulo, where I've just come from, you can buy it everywhere: canned, baked, boiled . . . Great for late night suppers when the fish aren't jumping.'

'Thank the stars we don't live in Tiabulo,' Dad whispered to Jack, behind his hand.

It was Sunday, and the family were sitting down to lunch. It was a late lunch because Uncle Joe had taken ages to cook it, but Tashi had only just arrived. He'd been making the dessert.

'Have you ever tried ghost pie?' asked Tashi. 'It's a secret recipe learned from ghosts I once knew.'

'No,' said Uncle Joe, 'but I remember a fortune teller once said – '

'Luk Ahed?' asked Jack.

'No, another one, in the Carribean Islands. Anyway, this man told me that when I was forty-three I would visit my brother and meet a wise young lad who would offer me a most mysterious dessert.'

'Luk Ahed shook his head sadly. "I'm sorry, Tashi, but we can't argue with destiny."

'"There must be something we can do. Couldn't *you* put in a good word for me?"

'Luk Ahed laughed unhappily. "*I'm* not important enough for that, Tashi. No, once your name has been written in the Great Book of Fate, there is nothing . . . " He paused. "Except your name hasn't been entered in the Book yet, has it? And it won't be written in until New Year's Eve . . . in two days' time. And if on that evening you were to . . . "

'I was beginning to notice that Luk Ahed had a very annoying habit of not finishing his sentences. "If I were to *what*, Luk Ahed?"

'Aha!' Dad smacked his forehead. 'Ghost pie! Eat a slice and walk through walls. What's more mysterious than that? Your fortune came true then, didn't it?'

'Sometimes it does,' Tashi said slowly, 'and sometimes it doesn't.'

Jack looked hard at Tashi. 'Did you go back and see *your* fortune teller?'

Tashi nodded. 'Yes, and it wasn't long before I wished I'd never stepped foot in the place.' He put his fork down. 'Luk Ahed had been so clever telling me about the magic shoes, I decided to visit him again. I thought maybe he'd find some more surprises in my horoscope.'

'And *did* he?' asked Dad eagerly.

'You can *bet* on it,' said Uncle Joe, playing hard with his peas. 'They always do.'

'More than I'd ever bargained for,' agreed Tashi. 'See, it was like this. Luk Ahed was just finishing his breakfast when I arrived, but he put down his pancake and licked his fingers. He was like that – always happy to see you, always eager to help. It was only a few days since my last visit to him, so my chart hadn't been completely buried under his books and papers.

'"Here it is!" he cried, pulling it out. He was so surprised and pleased with himself at finding it quickly that he did a little jig and almost upset his breakfast over the table. "Come and sit beside me on the bench while I read, Tashi," he invited.

'"Anyone who has already had such an exciting life as yours would be sure to have a very interesting future ahead of him."

'Well, I watched him read for a minute, and then suddenly he stopped smiling and covered his eyes with his hands.

'"Oh, Tashi," he said in a sorrowful voice.

'"What? What is it?"

'"Oh, Tashi, on the morning of your 10th birthday you are going to die!"

'"But that will be the day after tomorrow! Are you sure, Luk Ahed? I'm so healthy – look!" I jumped up and down and did one-arm push ups to show him I wasn't even breathing hard.

'The fortune teller was feverishly looking through his sacred books. "The Gods like to enjoy a particular meal on New Year's Eve," he said. "Very simple, but special. Each God has his own favourite dishes. Now, if we were to serve our God of Long Life his own personal special meal, cooked to perfection . . . "

'"He might put me back in the Book of Life!" I finished his sentence.

'"Exactly."'

'So what are the special dishes?' asked Uncle Joe. 'Not crocodile, by any chance? Braised perhaps, with noodles?'

'No,' Tashi shook his head. 'Wild mushroom omelette with nightingale eggs. Speckled trout with wine and ginger. And a bowl of golden raspberries.'

'Gosh!' said Dad. 'Where would you get a nightingale egg? *Are* there any in your part of the world, Tashi?'

'Not that I knew of – I'd never seen any nests in our forests. For a moment I did feel low, I can tell you. It all seemed impossible. But then I thought of my friend, the raven. He *had* said, "Just whistle if you ever need my help." Remember when he was hurt after that terrible storm, Jack? The night Baba Yaga blew in? And I knew the children I had rescued from the war lord would gladly gather the mushrooms for me. And Lotus Blossom's mother had a pond at the bottom of her house where I was almost *sure* I'd seen speckled trout swimming. Maybe it wasn't impossible after all.

'So I hastily said goodbye to Luk Ahed and ran home to the mulberry tree where the raven sometimes perched. He flew down at my second whistle and when I told him about the dinner and the nightingale eggs, he said, "Give me your straw basket and I will be back with them tomorrow."

'The village children were very excited when I explained about the mushroom.

'"We'll find enough for twenty Gods, Tashi," they shouted. Off they ran with their bags, clattering over the bridge into the fields and forest.

'Meanwhile, I hurried to Lotus Blossom's house. Her mother wasn't so happy to lose the beautiful speckled trout – they were her last three – but she gave a good-hearted smile as she scooped them out of her pond and handed them to me in a bowl of water.

'I raced back to the square where Luk Ahed stood, waving his hands. There was a great argument going on in the village about who would be the best people to cook the dishes. No one was listening to Luk Ahed, who was calling for order. Finally everyone agreed that Sixth Aunt Chow made the most delicious omelettes, but that Big Wu and his Younger Brother, Little Wu, should cook the fish.

'Next morning, cooking fires were set up in the square so everyone could watch and advise. The children were back before noon with beautiful baskets overflowing with four different kinds of mushrooms. In the early afternoon the raven returned. He looked quite bedraggled and tired, but in the basket were a dozen perfect nightingale eggs.

'Mrs Li brought out a bottle of her prized wine to add to the fish and I left them all busily chopping ginger roots and celery and bamboo shoots.

'Now the hardest task lay ahead. In all our province I had only ever seen one bush of golden raspberries. And it belonged to my enemy, the wicked Baron.'

'Oh, no!' cried Jack.

'Oh, yes!' said Tashi. 'I had brought my magic shoes with me but I decided not to put them on. As I walked slowly to his house I went over in my mind exactly *how* I would go about asking the Baron for a bowl of his berries.

'But I didn't have to ask. He had already heard the news and he was waiting for me with a fat smile on his face.

'"Well, Tashi," he gloated, "I hear that you are in need of some of my berries."

'"Yes, please."

'"Oh, you'll have to do much better than that." He shook a playful finger at me. "Something like this. Now, Tashi, say after me: Please, please most kindly, honourable and worthy Baron, could you give some berries to this miserable little worm Tashi, who stands before you?"

'I gritted my teeth and managed to force out the words, but the Baron pretended he couldn't hear and made me say it all over again. When I had finished, he thumped his fist on the table and shouted, "No, I couldn't! After all the trouble you have caused me, I'll be glad to be rid of you. Not a berry will you have."

'I was just leaving his house when Third Aunt called after me. She worked in the Baron's kitchen, remember, Jack? Well, she came close and whispered, "There *is* another bush of golden raspberries, Tashi. It belongs to the Old Witch who lives in the forest. But don't take any without asking her. The berries scream if anyone except the witch picks them."

'Oh dear, I didn't like the sound of that but what was I to do? It was the Old Witch's berries or none.

'This time I slipped my magic shoes on and I was in the forest in a few bounds. I found the Witch's cottage and there in the garden at the back of the house was a small raspberry bush. There were only a few golden berries on it but they looked round and juicy. I touched one gently and it gave a little scream.

'A door opened at once and a bony old
figure in a dusty black cloak came hobbling
down the path.

'"Who is meddling with my raspberry
bush?" she shrieked.

'She looked like a bunch of old broom sticks strung together. She was even more hideous than people had said. Her blackened teeth were bared in a fierce growl and her bristly chin was thrust out so far in rage that her beak almost touched it. I turned to run. I expected my magic shoes would take me to safety in one bound, but something in the way she stood there, alone on the garden path, made me stop. Her mouth puckered around her gums and her eyes were sad. Come to think of it, I had never heard of her harming anyone.

'I took a deep breath and said, "I was just looking at them, Granny, because I have a great need of golden raspberries at the moment."

'She cackled. "Oh, you have, have you?"
And she sat herself down on a bench. "Tell
me about it then."

'When I had finished, she pulled herself
up on my arm. She grinned at me, and with
her mouth no longer set in a growl and her
eyes sparkling with interest, she didn't look
nearly so scary. "Come on then," she said,
"we'll make a nice pot of tea and then you
can pick your berries. There aren't many
left but you'll find enough to fill a bowl,
I'm sure."

'You can imagine how joyfully I ran
back with my basket of fruit. But when
I reached the bridge by the Baron's house,
he was standing there, blocking my way.
His eyes bulged when he saw my berries
and with a roar of rage he charged towards
me and knocked the basket up in the air
and into the river. I hung over the railing
and watched in despair as the berries
bobbed away downstream.

'"How are you going to prepare your
wonderful meal now, eh, clever Tashi?" the
Baron sneered.

'I struggled to hold in my bitter feelings and faced him calmly. "We'll prepare the rest of the meal and I will take it to the mountain top, to the *Gods*, together with a note explaining that the delicious golden raspberries are missing because the wicked Baron, *YOU*, knocked them into the river."

'The Baron's jaw dropped and his mouth opened and closed. "That won't be necessary, my boy. Couldn't you see that I was just having a joke with you?"

'I folded my arms and said nothing
while the Baron pleaded with me to take all
the golden raspberries I needed.

'Finally, I shook my finger at him. "Oh,
you will have to do much better than that.
Now, Baron, say after me: Please, please
most kindly, honourable and worthy Tashi,
could you take the berries of this miserable
worm of a Baron, who stands before you?"

'The Baron gritted his teeth and forced
out the words. He even tried to smile as
I picked his fruit. I thanked him politely
for holding the basket for me.

'It was late afternoon by the time I got back to the village and everything was ready. A wonderful omelette filled with delicate flavoursome mushrooms lay on some vine leaves upon my mother's best platter. My mouth watered as I lifted the lid from the dish of speckled trout in wine and ginger and pickled vegetables that only Big Wu and Little Wu knew how to prepare. We washed the raspberries in fresh spring water, dried them and placed them gently in a moss-lined basket.

'Luk Ahed and I carried two baskets each and when we reached the mountain top, we spread out a gleaming white linen tablecloth and set out the meal. It was perfect.

'When it was nearly midnight we hid behind a tree and waited. On the stroke of twelve we were dazzled by a blinding silver light. We blinked against the light, closing our eyes for just a moment, but when we could see again the cloth was bare.

'Luk Ahed and I ran all the way back down the mountain and hurried to his house to see if my horoscope had changed. Luk Ahed peered at the chart, his brow wrinkling deeper with every second. I was holding my breath, and began to feel faint. If he didn't answer soon, I thought I might fall over and die right where I stood.

'"Tashi, the bad news is that all our work preparing that magnificent meal was for nothing."

'"!!!???!!!??"

'Then he smiled guiltily, bowing his head. "The *good* news is that you didn't need to do any of it. Look, here where I read *10th* birthday, it was really your *100th* birthday. You see, a little bit of breakfast pancake was covering the last zero."

'We stared at each other for a moment and began to laugh.

'"Let's not tell the village," said Luk Ahed. "They might be a little bit cross with me."'

The family looked at Tashi with their

mouths open. Uncle Joe's was still full of ghost pie, and a dollop fell out onto the table.

Jack cleared his throat. 'So how do you think you'll feel when you are nearly one hundred and you know you're going to die?'

'Oh,' Tashi waved airily, 'if I'm not quite ready, I'll just prepare another perfect meal for the God of Long Life.'

'Here's to a l-o-n-g friendship then,' said Uncle Joe, raising his glass of wine. They all clinked glasses and wished each other well. Then Uncle Joe added, 'You know, Tashi, that ghost pie really was excellent. It's given me a lot of energy. I think I'll go and stretch my legs after that long meal.' And he rubbed his hands together with excitement.

'It only lasts for three days!' Tashi called out, but Uncle Joe had already walked through the kitchen wall, and was gone.

'Great way to travel,' he yelled from the garden. 'See you soon!' And they heard him humming the old song, *'No walls can keep me in, no woman can tie me down, no jail can hold me now, da dum da dum da dum . . .'*

Tashi
and the
Dancing
Shoes

'The crowd gasped in amazement.
"Look at those shoes!
Look at him fly!"'

Jack's Uncle Joe loves to tell stories,
and so does Tashi – like the one
about the magic shoes and Uncle
Tiki Pu's sneaky plan…and what
Tashi did when the fortune teller,
Luk Ahed, said that his tenth
birthday would be his last.

There's no stopping Tashi.
Read all about his adventures
in the other *Tashi* books.

ALLEN & UNWIN

ISBN 1-74114-972-X

9 781741 149722

www.allenandunwin.c

Cover design by Sandra Nobes
Cover illustrations by Kim Gamble

FICTION